Anansi

Aurélien, Clara, Mademoiselle, and the English Lieutenant

ANNE HÉBERT

Aurélien, Clara, Mademoiselle, and the English Lieutenant

TRANSLATED BY
SHEILA FISCHMAN

Published in 1996 by
House of Anansi Press Limited
1800 Steeles Avenue West, Concord, ON
Canada L4K 2P3

First published in French as *Aurélien, Clara, Mademoiselle et
le Lieutenant anglais* in 1995 by
Éditions du Seuil

Distributed in Canada by
General Distribution Services Inc.
30 Lesmill Road
Toronto, Canada M3B 2T6
Tel. (416) 445-3333
Fax (416) 445-5967
e-mail: Customer.Service@ccmailgw.genpub.com

Distributed in the United States by
General Distribution Services Inc.
85 River Rock Drive, Suite 202
Buffalo, New York 14207
Toll free 1-800-805-1083
Fax (416) 445-5967
e-mail: Customer.Service@ccmailgw.genpub.com

Canadian Cataloguing in Publication Data

Hébert, Anne, 1916–
[Aurélien, Clara, Mademoiselle et le Lieutenant anglais. English]
Aurélien, Clara, Mademoiselle, and the English Lieutenant

Translation of: Aurélien, Clara, Mademoiselle et le Lieutenant anglais.
ISBN 0-88784-582-7

I. Title. II. Title: Aurélien, Clara, Mademoiselle et le Lieutenant anglais. English.

PS8515.E16A9713 1996   C843'.54   C96-930625-3
PQ3919.2.H42A9713 1996

Cover design: Bill Douglas @ The Bang
Computer layout: Mary Bowness
Printed and bound in Canada

*House of Anansi Press gratefully acknowledges the support of the Canada
Council and the Ontario Arts Council in the development of writing
and publishing in Canada.*

*This book was made possible in part through the Canada Council's
Translation Grants Program.*

Aurélien, Clara, Mademoiselle, and the English Lieutenant

I

IT HAPPENED ABRUPTLY, in lightning fashion. A sort of savage illumination struck Aurélien Laroche. In that harsh glare nothing of his old beliefs survived. Suddenly everything within him was devastated, like a field of grass delivered to the fire. Present, future, past, eternity — at one stroke all were abolished. Neither Christ nor the Church nor redemption nor the resurrection of the flesh: Aurélien had lost his faith the way a person loses the key to his house and can never go home again.

Aurélien was standing at the edge of the freshly filled-in grave, wearing his black suit for weddings and funerals, hat in his hand. It was July. The sun was beating down on his lowered eyelids. At his feet, flowers dusted with sand marked the place where his wife now rested, in the cemetery, next to the river.

The separation was now complete. All that remained was for Aurélien to trot back home at the leisurely pace of his old horse. At all costs he must avoid having all those people clustered behind him extend their hands and offer their condolences. His youthful face with its dried tears is no longer to be looked upon here until its final state of dead stone.

A house built of poorly squared planks, on the bank of the river. All around it, a sort of cage of thin grass. Obscure outbuildings, half-collapsed. Fields running close by the edge of the forest. From the road could be heard now and then the crying of Aurélien's child. In vain the village women offered to help: Aurélien chose to take care by himself of the small creature who had emerged from between the thighs of her dying mother in a fountain of blood.

Sometimes at night when Clara was asleep in her wooden cradle, a sort of evil shadow that did not belong to the night would circle the house, enter it, and make its way into Aurélien's chest, gripping his heart in a vise. He told himself then that he was locked within injustice, as if in a prison from which he would never be able to escape.

The days of diapers and bottles passed nearly without incident. Lines draped with baby clothes were hung once a week between two stunted trees.

The rest of the time, Clara, in her diapers, smelled very strongly of urine and of milk gone sour.

Aurélien took his daughter with him everywhere, rolled up in a faded sweater that had once been blue. He would lay her down in the grass in the shadow of the trees, under cheesecloth because of the mosquitoes, when he had to earth up plants or reap or plough. From time to time Aurélien would pick Clara up and hold her against his chest, to console her for being alone and so tiny, lost at the edge of a field or at the foot of a fir tree. He would decide on occasion to go to the village, do his errands with his daughter on his back, tied into the faded blue sweater, its sleeves knotted under Aurélien's chin.

With the image of his wife buried in the very marrow of his bones, all lament, all desolation forbidden him, Aurélien cared for his daughter and cared for his fields. The village people were kept at a distance in the same way as rebellion and tears.

Shaving before the pocked mirror above the kitchen sink, he would see his own face come to meet him like a taciturn stranger, and he would think about human dignity, which forbade him too much hidden aloofness or secret tumult.

Life flowed by, silent and monotonous, between the father and his child, along the bank of the river. It passed beneath the vast country sky, slack and bare, forever stripped of its angels and its saints. At no time would Aurélien, in the simplicity of his heart, dare to apply the name despair to the dark hole that moved along with him, under his feet, wherever he might be — in his house, on the road, or in the fields.

Clara grew up amid her father's silence and the voices of the countryside. Long before acquiring any human speech, the little girl could chirp, cackle, purr, coo, moo, bark, and yelp. Her imitation of the great horned owl when dusk had fallen was so true that the blood of the field mice froze in their veins.

Sometimes Clara would surrender herself to the trills of birds known to her alone, so limpid and pure that she would abruptly fall silent, choked with happiness.

"What an opera singer my Clara could be," thought Aurélien, having picked up the word "opera" long ago, during a conversation he overheard at the general store between the notary's wife and a passing traveller.

At the age of ten Clara was unable to read or write and her vocabulary was as limited as that of a child of three.

— THREE TIMES ALREADY the new village schoolmistress had come to fetch Clara and take her to school. Just out of normal school, her zeal was extreme, and she taught her class as if the salvation or damnation of every one of her pupils depended on her good will.

The schoolmistress had frothy red hair that made a halo around her in the sun, and gold-rimmed spectacles that gave off flashes whenever she moved her head. She sat very erect in the cluttered kitchen while some round-eyed white hens pecked beneath the table that was never cleared. The schoolmistress accepted the glass of dandelion wine Aurélien offered her, drained it in one gulp, wiped her lips with an embroidered handkerchief, and began to extol the benefits of school for children. According to her, all the knowledge in the world was to be found collected in texts and exercise books, coloured maps that hung on the wall, and on the enormous blackboard which was gradually inscribed with the rapid signs of knowledge on the march.

It was a whitewashed village school, under a pinnacle of grey shingles, and in it children of good will were promised that they would possess the earth.

"You understand, Monsieur Laroche, your daughter is as beautiful as the sun and moon combined, but the mind inside that curly head lies fallow, fallow . . ."

She repeated "fallow" despairingly, and Clara thought she could hear beneath the leaves the muffled lament of an animal unknown to her. And then it occurred to Aurélien that the entire earth was lying fallow, resembling in that way his own fields filled with rocks and sand, as well as the devastated sky above his head and his heart, which was equally mute and stony. He asked himself if it was good for his daughter to leave abruptly the deep dark life where things are never expressed or named, to go and lose herself in a garrulous and pretentious world. At the same time, though, Aurélien was filled with pride because the teacher had acknowledged Clara's beauty and had compared her with the sun and moon.

As for Clara, from the schoolmistress's first visit she was dazzled by the light that glinted from the young woman's red hair, from her gold-rimmed glasses, and from the rings she wore on both her right hand and her left — rings that wedded her to all the earth.

And as the teacher spoke, all her unfamiliar and mysterious words were charged with the same gilt and reddish radiance, so superb one could die from it.

Soon Clara had but one thought, to learn to read and write and count, simply so she could spend the day under the influence of that radiant redness.

After several days of grim reflection, Aurélien finally gave in to his daughter's pleas. The next day he bought her patent-leather shoes with straps so she could make her entrance into the school. Very soon it turned out that Clara's feet, accustomed to running about quite bare, could not tolerate the fine shoes Aurélien had bought. She carried them all the way from the house to the village and only put them on once she was within sight of the school, and she entered it very erect, standing firmly in her shiny shoes.

Seated in the first row with the youngest nursery-school pupils, facing Mademoiselle, fiercely flashing, Clara learned to read and write in record time. It seemed to her she had to run with all her might across shifting ice that was constantly threatening to shatter. Even more than the tiny black letters in her reader that she gradually deciphered, Clara loved the ringing sound of the new words in her teacher's mouth, as if she were discovering some new music that enchanted her.

One day, when the little girl had worked particularly well, Mademoiselle took her white hand bedecked with rings and lifted Clara's face up to her own, gazing very deeply into her eyes, and she murmured so softly that only Clara could hear her, as in a dream:

"In the depths of those eyes, *the river is deep and all the king's horses could drink there together.*"

These remarkable words, like a sigh against Clara's cheek, scarcely surprised her, so certain was she that all the wonders in the world would soon be revealed to her. For were not the king's horses and the king himself, wearing his crown, advancing solemnly from the end of the horizon on their way to her, to drink from the pupils of her own dark eyes?

Time seemed suspended between Clara and Mademoiselle. The entire class, from nursery school to fourth grade, became more and more agitated, buzzing like a flight of hornets. Mademoiselle, bending over Clara, did not speak and did not stir. Clara came to fear her teacher's stillness, her feverish pallor which she now saw up close, with the freckles drifting across her linen-white skin.

The little girl lowered her gaze and for a long time she concentrated on the knots in the wide boards at her feet.

While Clara had easily won the admiration of the nursery-school pupils, thanks to some ringing imitations of roosters at sunrise and of barn swallows at sunset, such was not the case with the older students at the back of the classroom. Girls and boys were constantly nudging each other and snickering because Clara's dresses, which were too short for her, resembled faded calico sacks, her unkempt hair a blackbird's nest after a storm. But what soon proved to be the last straw for the class, the older children and the younger ones united in their resentment, was their certainty that Mademoiselle's lessons were now addressed only to Clara. Numbers, letters, words, whole sentences now flew over their heads, floating in the stuffy air of the schoolroom like a wild swarm that had broken free, to settle solely on Clara's mop of tow-coloured hair.

For the teacher it was a question of delivering

to the daughter of Aurélien Laroche, as quickly as possible, before it was too late, all the knowledge stored up in her blazing red head.

Clara, for her part, was keenly aware of her teacher's urgency. Her intelligence was wakened at the speed of the day when it emerges from the darkness, then climbs to the horizon, leaps across the pebbles on the river's banks, skips over the dark crest of the trees, gallops full speed across the water's flat surface, intoxicated by its own movement, by its singular dazzle, as it emerges from the night.

Though Clara did not leave her place among the nursery-school children in the first row, very close to Mademoiselle's platform, after two years she reached the point where she could share the lessons and homework of the grade four pupils at the back of the class, where there were mainly girls, since schooling beyond grade three was considered by the parents to be something that might unman their big boys.

Often Mademoiselle kept Clara after class, explaining to her very quickly problems that had to do with faucets and trains, then lingering briefly over the agreement of participles before moving on to fables and tales, sometimes even progressing to poems, while her cheeks were stained with red and her voice became increasingly choked.

One winter night, when darkness had long since fallen and the fire in the schoolroom stove died out completely, and Clara was ready to leave, with her tuque on and her coat buttoned up to her chin, she gathered up her courage and decided to speak to her teacher. All in one breath, with her eyes fixed obstinately on the floor, she said that this could not go on, this haste, this extreme impatience, this lack of time in which they were both trapped, she said that this was no way to live, that she could not breathe, and that it frightened her. Saying this, Clara dropped her head lower and lower, as if some explanation of the mysteries of this world would come to her from the wide grey boards that lay barely touching at her feet. Soon the young girl had lost her voice and she finished her tirade in a nearly inaudible gasp.

"Why are you in such a hurry, Mademoiselle, why? Will you go away soon and leave me all alone in my house by the river, with the cries of animals and the songs of birds?"

Mademoiselle shuddered under her black woollen shawl, a little as if an icy weapon had touched her back between the shoulder-blades.

"I need to tell you everything I know, give you everything I have. It is like a legacy I want to leave you."

"Are you going away then?"

Two small red circles appeared very clearly on Mademoiselle's pale cheeks, like make-up applied with too heavy a hand. Clara thought this sudden redness was caused by her teacher's bewilderment at the thought of a mysterious journey of which she could not speak.

"I don't want you to go away!"

As she cried out, Clara's voice had the tone, familiar and harsh, of the inhabitants of Sainte-Clotilde.

Mademoiselle pulled Clara's woollen tuque further down over her ears and told her that she should leave, that it was very late.

Once she was on the road home, which followed the frozen river, amid the vast solitude of a winter night wherein the only sign of life was a thin thread of water that glistened black in the middle of the current, Clara found herself regretting the fact that Mademoiselle had never taught her how to ward off the ill fortune that was moving through the snow-covered countryside, in the very heart of the shadows, where there were neither moon nor stars.

Mademoiselle lifted her two diaphanous hands into the light; one after the other she pulled off all her rings and let them fall onto the little iron bed edged with flowered cretonne. She said to Clara:

"Pick the rings up. All of them. They're for you. It's all for you. Books, linen, dresses, everything. The others will have nothing."

Clara asked who these others were. Mademoiselle shrugged her shoulders, as if she considered the question to be annoying.

"The others, all the others, the family, every last one of them. They'll have nothing. Only you."

And at the same time she was saddened to be reduced to material gifts, with nothing left to offer from her country schoolmistress's mind. Had she not already given Clara everything — reading and writing, arithmetic and sacred history, even stories and poems that were not on the curriculum but were the very substance of the singular flame that was burning inside her?

It was then that Mademoiselle thought of the recorder as her supreme offering, the little instrument she sometimes played when she was alone, that she carefully concealed under piles of linen in the fir chest of drawers.

Clara was in Mademoiselle's bedroom for the first time, and she was astonished to find it so cold and bare.

"I must teach you how to play the recorder,

this minute, this very minute! I forgot to teach you to play it!"

The schoolmistress sat on the floor, her back against the wall. Little by little the circulation was restored to her icy fingers and her harsh breathing softened, became pure and limpid. It was as though the voice of an angel were bursting from the magical instrument, to the amazement of Clara who had never heard anything like it.

All this was taking place in the dead of winter, in the snow-covered countryside around Sainte-Clotilde, in the heart of the schoolmistress's little bedroom adjoining the village school. The schoolmistress who now was crumbling like a dead leaf.

Day by day, Clara was learning to play the instrument. Mademoiselle was growing more and more exhausted and her breath had the taste of fever.

When the little girl knew how to produce a tune, how to modulate and to play trills and runs quite easily, Mademoiselle said that her days as a teacher were now at an end and that she had nothing more to give Clara, save her living woman's vermilion blood, and that soon it would be done. Saying this, she smiled. Clara had hardly enough time to be astonished at so strange an utterance

16

when already her teacher had taken to her bed to die, half-sitting, with her back propped against a pile of pillows.

The death throes lasted all day and all night. Clara watched over Mademoiselle, wiping the sweat from her forehead, the blood from her mouth. Clara thought about the shattered order of the world, about her mother who had died giving her life. Twice begotten, by two different women, Clara secretly weighed the twofold mystery of her mingled legacy.

Mademoiselle's sisters, who arrived the next day, at first resembled her like three peas in a pod, with their russet hair and their gold-rimmed spectacles. Little by little, each of them took on a fierce expression that did not evoke Mademoiselle at all. Little red-headed vultures, for had they not come to observe that nothing was left of their youngest sister's belongings, neither in the drawers of the fir chest, nor in the battered old raffia trunk, nor on the roughly peeled wooden shelf, nor behind the door where big black nails had been planted for clothes to hang on? Clara had taken everything away with her to her father's house on the bank of the river, according to her teacher's wish.

Her name was Blandine Cramail. She was nineteen years old. Sainte-Clotilde was her first post. It was said in the village that the schoolmistress had been carried off by galloping consumption.

Clara did not attend the ceremony in the Sainte-Clotilde church. She stood at her window, unmoving, her face turned towards the church, while the bells tolled the knell. When silence had been restored to the countryside, in the way that ice re-forms and solidifies from one end of the world to the other, Clara improvised funeral music on her recorder, so heartbreaking and pure that Aurélien's walled-up sorrow erupted again as it had in the early days of his widowerhood. Then there was only a single mourning, celebrated by the sound of a recorder: that of the father and of his daughter, on the frozen earth on the bank of a white river, like a field where white foam had been spilled.

II

— IN THE HEART of the day, the heart of the night, time passes. On the river, in the fields and the woods, birth and death reign in equal measure, with no beginning and no end, from the minuscule mayflies skating across the river on long thin legs that dissolve at once into the blue air, to the children of men who are astonished at the speed of the light as it makes its way towards the darkness.

Clara's age changed so quickly that she scarcely had time to carve it with her knife, along with the date, on a heavy brown beam above her bed in her attic bedroom, amid the garlands of onions hung on the walls and the shrivelled, sour little apples that sat on the sill of the dormer window.

Twelve years, thirteen, fourteen. Soon, she will be fifteen years old.

Clara no longer reads tales or poems. She no longer reviews in her head the knowledge bequeathed by her teacher. Clara is bored.

For a long time, when the wind blew in the evening, Mademoiselle's dresses would sway gently where they hung on the wall near the poorly sealed dormer window, breathing in the shadows and seemingly alive. And now little by little Mademoiselle's dresses are losing their colour and becoming as thin as onionskin. The day is approaching when the very image of Mademoiselle in Clara's memory will become like a coin that has grown faded and worn until it is no longer legal tender.

Clara did the laundry for women from town who spent the summer in Sainte-Clotilde, and hung it on long cords stretched between two trees; she cared for the animals, hoed the garden, and prepared the meals.

In the evening, taking shelter in her attic, she would sometimes feel in her entire weary body how deeply she resembled the grass and trees, the animals and fields and all that lives and dies, without complaining or breaking any silence.

Some evenings, though, when the newborn moon, red as a sun, spread out in broad streaks across the river, Clara's heart would leap in her chest, would pound against her ribs as if it wanted to break out and roam the world. Under the russet moon the earth's beauty would weigh down on Clara, seeming to demand that her life burst outside her and that she offer up entirely her remarkable and fierce little self.

And then Clara would sometimes play the recorder late at night, sitting on the grass beside the river. She would go through her entire repertoire, and when she ran out of pieces to play, she would improvise strange, strident music that would rend the air around her.

Aurélien would put his hands to his ears then and beg for mercy. He wanted nothing so much as for ordinary life to resume its course, calm and monotonous, both inside his own house and over all his sandy, rocky land. Above all else, he liked evenings without music, when Clara would prepare food and drink and set it on the table before him, with no useless words or gestures.

As she was then during the childhood that wears out and worsens, Clara would remain the salt of Aurélien's life.

— For two years now, war was being fought in the old countries on the other side of the Atlantic Ocean. And at this moment, signs of that war could be discerned even in the countryside around Sainte-Clotilde, on the opposite bank of the river, where a military camp was going up at Valcour not far from the house of Aurélien Laroche.

Whenever Clara happened to be travelling around the countryside on her father's old bicycle, she had to give wide berth to the soldiers scattered along the road and to the trucks with their right-hand drive.

They would materialize here and there, in twos or in small groups. They spoke English or French. Called her "darling" or "*chérie*." They would invite her to go to bed with them. But Clara merely greeted them, very softly, without moving her lips. "Hello, hello all you men who are watching for me along the road like cats watching for a mouse, let me by, I'm not for you, not for you handsome gentlemen in your khaki shorts, raised in a military camp amidst all sorts of murderous weapons that could mortally wound any girl in the countryside around Sainte-Clotilde who found herself in your way."

Then Clara would pedal away on her bicycle as if she had an appointment to keep beyond the horizon, on the other side of the mountain stripped bare by firing exercises.

There are so many wild strawberries that summer, they don't know what to do with them. Clara spends long hours crouched in the grass by the fields, close to the fragrant earth that exhales its warm breath onto her face. From morning to night, to say nothing of the noon-hour when the Angelus drops its clear notes onto the mountain brimming with fire, Clara picks the berries that are hidden under the leaves. Every evening, she brings home big buckets filled with carefully hulled fruit. Her red-stained hands seem not to belong to her.

"A dollar a bucket! A quarter a box!"

Clara sells strawberries to ladies from town who are on vacation in Sainte-Clotilde. Hunched over her bicycle, its baggage-carrier laden with boxes, she travels through the countryside riddled with sun, her nape roasted, and her arms and calves. That sweatiness in her hair.

She comes and goes from one house to the next. Her hoarse voice, half-swallowed, barely audible, tirelessly spouts her song: "A dollar a bucket! A quarter a box!"

No cool spot anywhere in the countryside. The dry shade spread along the road in broad deceptive patches hardly less blazing than the shimmering sun. Customers are increasingly rare, the houses farther and farther apart, nestled under the trees.

Here the road is so narrow that the trees' shadows seem to touch above her head. A thin thread of unshaded light still persists on the sand in the middle of the road, where Clara has been pedalling ceaselessly since morning. Something stronger than the wind — though wind is absent from the heat-numbed countryside — urges her along on her clattering bicycle, forces her to go deeper into this unknown country.

It is no small thing to cross through the absolute newness of the air along a deserted road,

27

to breathe great gusts of it, of this air that has never been breathed before, to sense its resistance with each turn of the wheel, to feel its warm breath over every inch of her skin.

It cannot continue like this, this midday with no point of reference, always advancing but arriving nowhere, pushed from behind and urged to cross the line of the horizon.

Fir trees and spruce, as far as the eye can see, choking each other, and here and there a solitary pine, nearly transparent tamaracks, a few birches on puddles of green moss. The vast murmur of July rises from all sides at once. Thousands of wild little voices accompany Clara, deafen her, merge with the giddiness of the sun.

◆ TREES WITH FRESHLY lopped branches, their wounds white in the harsh light, are a sign that someone has only recently carved this path out of the forest. Clara did not see the mailbox at the edge of the ditch, half buried in the undergrowth, with a foreign name written there in capital letters. Now she is setting her foot on the ground, pulling her heavy bicycle like a horse by its bridle and entering the path where pebbles and tree roots are strewn on the surface of the earth.

Amid the chirping of crickets, the fragrance of resinous trees warmed by the sun, the odour of yellow and russet needles turned over beneath her feet, Clara continues making her way. Her bicycle tires leave sinuous traces on the sand behind her that are soon erased.

All at once, the desolation of the little log camp, blackened and rusty from inclement weather, is there before her, in the centre of a tiny glade that has been barely cleared. Clara realizes at once that the river is nearby and that reassures her, like a familiar presence.

Her vigilant blackbird's gaze looks all around, peers at the rare trampled grass, the fresh stumps, the still unpeeled tree-trunks, the branches covered with dried and curled-up leaves, a cord of wood stacked carefully next to the little camp with its closed windows.

And now she turns on her heels and sees him, sees a man sleeping in a canvas chair. She takes her time to look at him while he cannot yet see her. He is stunned by the heat, with a book open on his lap, his unseeing face offered to the sun. She stares at him shamelessly, the part of her that is still a child urging her to study thoroughly and unblinkingly all the visible and invisible things in this world.

She sees him now as she will never be able to see him again, with the freedom of the first glance, all the while judging him severely. Tall, thin, bony, bare-chested, khaki shorts, this man who is dry like a flower pressed inside a missal resembles those soldiers hungry for girls and alcohol who travel around at the heart of the day, fair weather and foul, along the narrow roads from Valcour to Sainte-Clotilde.

No doubt she should not let her footsteps decide for her and bring her so close to the sleeping man; this has nothing to do with her, or so it appears. Now she examines him as if through a lens. This man's solitude, as he lies here abandoned to sleep, is exposed to the devouring sunlight. His ribs, visible beneath the suntanned skin, rise slowly, the heartbeat of his life laid bare, and Clara is unable to move, caught as she is in a kind of distraction that will never leave her again. From now on, without thought or reflection, she will be reduced to the movement of the earth's blood within her and around her in the countryside.

What the sleeper sees inside the darkness of his night, under his closed eyelids, will never be revealed to Clara during the brief acquaintanceship they will subsequently share. Only barely does she become aware of the invasion of fear on the foreign face that undergoes a change as he dreams in her presence. Presently he trembles so hard that she will have no peace until she makes him emerge from his night. Very softly she calls to him:

"Monsieur! Monsieur! You're dreaming!"

He wakes with a start, shrinks back towards his house until he can feel the poorly squared tree-trunks against his thin back. He says *"My God"* in his language and his gaze measures the narrow space that separates him from this little girl, who is staring at him like some strange animal.

She does not move, she is rooted to the spot. Her eyes like lustrous coals. Her faded calico dress, long in the back, short in front, reveals her knees.

"*My-God-my-Lord-goddamn*," says the Lieutenant in one breath, in a single devastating word.

And he moves towards Clara. His long dry body folds like a breaking tree, leans up against her. The heat of the sun on the Lieutenant's skin envelops her in a deadly and powerful smell. She sees from very close the long hands covered with blisters.

Caught in the act of dreaming and dread, he apologizes with foreign words she does not understand.

"I apologize for the fear on my face and the shame of the fear on my damn body, it was only a nightmare, dear child."

He says *nightmare* again and laughs a great thunderous laugh. He pulls on his shirt and picks up his dark glasses that have fallen in the grass.

From this moment, Clara will no longer see the Lieutenant's pale eyes. Scarcely does she notice at times her own oddly shaped image reflected in his glasses as in a distorting mirror.

He takes a long look at the chalky sky through his dark glasses, one injured hand shielding his eyes. He says "Hush," one finger to his lips. He seems to be waiting for something to shatter and break in the overly calm sky. He says in an overseas French, learned in the region of Tours, that one must never trust the gentleness of the sky and that the fire is hissing and spitting, every night that the good Lord brings us, in the sky over London. Then it turns so bright above the city gleaming with light that you could thread a needle with your eyes closed, as long as you do not tremble, of course. *To tremble or not to tremble, that is the question.*

In the sultry air all around them, like stagnant water which they swallow and breathe at the risk of losing their footing, the Lieutenant's laughter bursts out again and then abruptly cracks.

She continues to stand motionless and mute before him, an entire line of ancestors rushing through her veins and forbidding her any fury or exultation, save for prayer or blasphemy.

"You're not very talkative, my dear!"

The Lieutenant's English voice is deep, as if it were emerging from his belly. Again he peers at the sky overhead.

"There's a storm heading our way," he says.

Clara raises her eyes towards the sky that has started turning white like a blister and shakes her head, No.

"Are you afraid of storms?"

Again she shakes her head, even though she feels as if she is lying, and suddenly she fears the storm more than anything else in the world.

The Lieutenant's fine heavy voice deteriorates, resembles the drone of an insect shut up in a jar.

"How old are you?"

"In two months I'll be fifteen."

He tells her he likes that and laughs, half hidden behind his dark glasses. The only light in his dark face is the dazzle of his white teeth.

The Lieutenant abruptly stops laughing, as if he has been ordered to be silent in the stifling air.

Now she asks for something to drink.

He goes to fetch a glass of water and he waits until she has finished drinking. She clinks the ice, surprised at the mist on the glass, having never seen ice cubes in a glass. She takes pleasure in leaving the warm mark of her fingers on it.

Now the Lieutenant has only one thought in mind: that this little girl who is lingering here should disappear as quickly as possible. For it is the Lieutenant's most fervent wish to be again as he was before her appearance, utterly alone and non-existent, stretched out in his canvas chair like a dead man, delivered up to the sun here in this place, which under his closed eyelids could almost be fire set loose in the sky over London.

This time the Lieutenant's voice is nothing more than a breath that she reads on his lips rather than hears:

"You should go home now, right away, or you'll get a scolding."

The Lieutenant gestures broadly with both arms. He points to Clara's buckets and boxes, scattered over the grass.

"I'll buy it all!"

She has gathered up her empty buckets and boxes and mounted her bicycle and now she is pedalling into the dying sun, the shadows all but imperceptible at the feet of the trees.

On the return trip as on the outward journey, she is surrounded by the rumour of July. Along both sides of the road, myriad voices form her retinue. Crickets and locusts drone, here and there the acid song of the cicada rises in the air, and on powerful wingbeats comes the call of an invisible bird.

And now these many familiar voices and the blazing vibration of the air withdraw all at once, like the ebbing tide, while the Lieutenant's foreign voice fills the space, seems to well up from everywhere at once, along the ditches, on the grass of the embankments, and in the distance, behind the edge of the woods, deep inside the moss and underbrush.

His voice, nothing but the Lieutenant's voice, its hoarse foreign sweetness lacking in sense, with no perceptible words, only the enchantment of his voice, accompanies Clara long after she has taken her leave of him.

Not until she has crossed the bridge over the river and passed through the village is the song of the earth around Clara reduced once more to a chirring of insects along the side of the road, into a confused murmur in the countryside.

➤ WIELDING THE AXE until his strength was exhausted, he has carved into the countryside. Fifty feet long by fifty feet across. He has appropriated for himself the little abandoned log camp on the bank of the river. He has cleared the view onto the river. During all the time that he will pass among us he will not unpack his valise, which sits on the ground, wide open, between the camp cot and the deal chest of drawers. See him now on his knees on the floor, rummaging in the tangle of his clothes, searching for flasks and bandages. His hands are covered with resin, with gum, and with the blisters he has just burst that now are oozing. He wraps his hands like Jesus and waits until it is fully dark before lighting the gas lamp that sits on the table.

Someone who is invisible in the shadows, mingled with the indistinct breath of the shadows, murmurs that this child is really too self-indulgent, and that this must change.

Sitting there into the night, on a kitchen chair in the middle of his one room, any voices or whispers having retreated to the four corners of the shadows, little by little John Christopher Simmons is filled with the silent night, filled to the brim, passive as a bucket plunged into black water.

Soon it will be possible for him, here in this silence, to feel the forest that is coming closer to the little camp, slowly encircling it; one day it will take back the land that has been cleared all around it, like its own sovereign possession, ravaged by the violence of the axe and of the furious man who held it.

He had not known that he possessed such fury and resentment against the trees.

One day the grown-ups rose in a tall forest at the heart of a noble dwelling in the West End. Their horrified faces could be seen hoisted to the summits of enormous tree trunks. Amid the foliage of the ceiling their dark faces were uncovered, bent over a scrawny little boy only to reproach or to show wrath. Nurses and governesses, tutors and chambermaids, cooks, butlers, chauffeurs formed an endless hedge in the Lieutenant's memory, standing there to welcome solemnly the parents of the little boy who were moving forward now, overflowing with fierce energy and equine odours.

All must be felled, must be prevented from growing back, the pines, the firs, the spruce, and the birch, all around the log cabin, to ensure the space he needs for his ruminations, here in this land of exile. So thinks the Lieutenant as he lies on his narrow bed, an army blanket drawn up over his face. While set loose forever in his veins, despite space and time, a British child tries to hide his frightened face beneath the authorities' reproachful gazes.

"That child is afraid of his own shadow, we'll never make a man of him."

Born into fear, brought up under the shame of fear as beneath a she-wolf who might have nourished him, now he lies on a camp cot in a god-forsaken cabin, on Canadian soil, thinking he is safe in the dark, breathing the cabin's musty air, sensing the field mice nibbling under the floor.

"If the lad falls off his horse we shall put him back in the saddle at once, despite his cries and his tears, so he will learn that fear, like hunger and thirst, heat and cold, can be controlled and ordered at will."

Wherever he goes, whatever he does, the Lieutenant is always being put on trial. From beyond the ocean he has crossed, from the very end of the British Isles now left behind forever, come to him voices of majesty and authority telling him over and over that he is a coward.

Already he has twice gone to the window and pulled the cretonne curtain over the pane, as if re-creating the blackout, as strictly as possible. It would take only a hole in the curtain, an infinitesimal tear, and the blitz would be visible again, released into the darkness. Horror and folly. This night is flawless, utterly black, calm, warm, and soft. He may as well get used to the goodness of the world and roll himself up in it as if it were a blanket.

The Lieutenant climbs back into his bed only inches off the floor, where he can hear close at hand the mice that squeak and nibble more vigorously than ever, as if their days were numbered.

An ancient and tiny terror. Now the Lieutenant is moving his bed so he won't hear the mice.

English courage has no example in the world but English courage, that's well known; the Lieutenant snickers, his head in his pillow, while the whole family council assembles in his head, to judge him and condemn him.

"Lieutenant, miraculously or inadvertently this lad has been lost to England's honour. Anyone who has seen him in a local shelter during a bombing raid can testify to that. Tears and fits of hysterics. We shall send him away to regain his health, *out of this world of sound and fury.* The Commonwealth is great. Surely we'll be able to find a peaceful part of it where he can pursue his military service in perfect tranquillity."

From his first day on Canadian soil, the Lieutenant knew that nothing was finished, knew that everything was beginning again as if he had not crossed the Atlantic, as if the savage expression that passed over his face was the same as the London smog on the nights of bombardments.

It took just one normal day at the military camp in Valcour. The ravaged hills of the firing range, the smoke escaping from the mortars, the detonations rending the air, the military orders like streams of abuse shouted by officers and NCOs. And life had become intolerable again.

It was he who chose this refuge in the middle of the woods, along the river between Valcour and Sainte-Clotilde. Neither radio nor newspapers, a woman to clean every Thursday, auburn and plump, pallid and strewn with freckles, who gripes and who blithely breaks the few dishes put at the Lieutenant's disposal. Too much noise. The woman makes too much noise. And she's too fat. In a little while he will send her away, as he himself was sent away from England and from the military camp at Valcour. Let each person remain ashamed to be hunted down. For in the secrecy of his soul each has good reason for his shame and for being hunted down. This morning, for instance, that little girl dismissed from the sight of his man's face, her hands red from berry-picking, her eyes open too wide, her entire slim, hard body no doubt already suffering the ravages of the menstrual flow. Too many grown-ups in the world. Too many little girls who cross the frontier and meet up with the cohort of grown-ups who are huge and without pity. Only little girls with smooth bellies, asleep amid their rumpled wings, can lay claim to the sweetness of the world.

He opens the plank door that gives on to the river and the night. Breathes deeply. There is no salt in this air, it is muggy and pervasive, like water that is too soft. It is pointless to live here, in parentheses, separated from everything. Life here, life there, like two sections of the Red Sea that has been parted to allow the Lieutenant's boundless solitude to pass.

The heat persists though it is night, it has stopped moving, is slow and viscous, flows between the trees, through their needles and leaves, it floats upon the river.

Sweltering heat like that in a steam room fills the enclosed space where one must, after all, live until tomorrow.

Even before dawn comes to light up the black sky, the birds have begun cheeping very softly and a muted rain has started to fall, small, wide-spaced drops, clearly perceptible but hard as pearls spilled onto the leaves and the log roof.

The Lieutenant listens to the rain fall, distinguishes each drop, each hard pearl in the noisy air, his hearing increasingly keen and quick, suddenly alert and awake, eager to know what kind of day it will be.

Soon everything grows hazy in the countryside and in the Lieutenant's ears. He has shut the door behind him and now he is alone, in the middle of a violent downpour that is coming from everywhere at once, pouring onto the roof, beating against the windows, streaming in rivulets onto the floor.

Little by little the smell of damp earth penetrates the Lieutenant's house, seeps into his clothes, clings to his skin. The furious summer rain awakens the black heart of the earth, pulls from its entrails its primeval breath, fills the Lieutenant's nostrils, his throat and his skinny chest. In the same way, the little strawberry-picker yesterday was as fragrant as the earth, filled with wild scents beneath her faded calico skirt, every time she moved under the intolerable sun. Nothing else to report. He does not even know her name.

The next day, Thursday, John Christopher Simmons dismissed the woman who cleans his house.

— FOR SEVERAL DAYS Clara is unable to go back to the Lieutenant's house because of the storms. She uses that time to tidy the house (as if she were leaving on a journey), and starts mending and darning, while violet glimmers rap at the windows to enter the kitchen, and the river studded with lightning rises before her very eyes.

This girl would like to play the flute amid the storm and the desolation, but she is unable to do so. What is inside her resembles nothing that is known and it ravages her like a fever that cannot be expressed in words or in music. At this very moment something is being decided in the rain-drenched countryside, something deaf and blind and terribly opaque, of which she can see neither the beginning nor the end, and which concerns her. If she should happen to lift her head from her work, it is to look out the window at the river rising in the rain, like someone spying from the corner of her eye a pan of milk that is boiling over on the stove.

Long attentive to the disasters inside him and around him, Aurélien peers out at his garden and his flooded fields. Has on his hat, his old jacket. Rain is falling onto his face, running down his neck and inside his sleeves. Endlessly he checks the level of the river. Aurélien has planted a post on the bank and he waits for it to be completely submerged or swept away by the current. He is apprehensive about the moment when he will have to make a decision about the imminent disaster caused by the rising water.

She is the only daughter and he the only father, and she is making ready to betray him in secret.

Accustomed since childhood to this rumbling of the water at her door, day after day, more powerful or less, more lilting or less, at times elusive and disappearing suddenly amid the regular respiration of the earth, then coming back in force very close to her ear and enchanting her again, Clara has come to confuse the beating of her own life with the river's rise and fall. And now she is astonished at her inner confusion and tumult, which are reflected in the eddies in the rising river.

Clara's hands grow languid as she works, and she lets them drop side by side onto her knees like two small animals that have been killed. Naïve as the angel ruffling the feathers of his white wings in the sunlight, her heart is filled with dark zones that disturb her. She tries to take her own inventory, in order to see a little more clearly in the growing night. She is thinking very hard, as if she were carefully writing in a schoolgirl's scribbler.

My name is Clara Laroche.
I am nearly fifteen years old.
My father, Aurélien Laroche, a farmer at
Sainte-Clotilde, is a widower, my mother
having died when I was born.
I know how to read, write and count.
Everything I know I was taught by Mademoiselle,
who is dead.
I weigh about one hundred pounds.
I stand five feet and some inches.
I am growing before your very eyes,
I am dark as a crow,
I play the recorder.
I think I've fallen in love with the English
Lieutenant.

Seeing her so absorbed and so remote, so near to being lost in thought, Aurélien cannot help asking his daughter the question he has always been careful not to ask, one he could not bear to be asked himself.

"What are you thinking about?"

"Nothing, really, nothing."

Saying that she lowers her eyes, sticks her needle again and again into the coarse fabric of an old skirt; her mouth is shut, her eyes closed, and her heart is brimming with uncontainable joy.

Thinking of his harvest that is rotting where it stands, Aurélien has gone outside to look at the disaster. The door slams behind him.

Clara has not stopped sewing. Each small stitch, even and straight, that she tirelessly sews in the cloth seems to be speaking in her stead, repeating like a monotonous litany: "I'll do it. I'll do it. I'll do it."

After she has cut the thread with her teeth, she lifts her shining face from her work. She looks at the blank wall before her and murmurs, talking to herself, as if she cannot help it, her voice hushed, softly, for herself alone, each syllable standing out from the others, holding back her laughter as the amazing words are whispered into the silence of the empty kitchen: "I'll do it. I'll do it. I'll do it. I will be the wife of the English Lieutenant."

She is astonished that she wants it so badly, as if her life depended on it.

That evening in her attic, she stands for a long moment undecided before Mademoiselle's dresses hanging on the wall, like a woman choosing a dress in a shop who does not know which to select. Clara finally decides on the most beautiful one, both skirt and top a slightly faded red, with bursts of colour deep in the folds. She spreads the dress on a chair, placed on the floor next to the chair the high-heeled patent-leather shoes. For a long time she has been holding a tiny lipstick in a golden case that turned up in a surprise package she'd been given at the general store.

Beneath the downpour tumbling from the sky and against the earth that steams from its own warm breath for long days still, coming and going from the house to the outbuildings and from the out-buildings to the house, Clara is now waiting only for good weather, like a fiancée who has secretly pre-pared her finery, who goes about her usual business and now, in her head, is counting the hours until her wedding day.

Sometimes at night she gets up to look out her dormer window at the rainwater that can no longer disappear into the earth, that is creating a slack lake around the house.

⟶ HE SAW THE bright sky move across the country-side. He shaved closely then, sprinkled himself generously with rainwater from head to toe, donned fresh clothes and waited until the fine weather had fully arrived.

There are still too many vague glimmers hanging in the electric air for the Lieutenant to feel truly at peace. It would take only one small match held high above his head for the entire sky to be set ablaze once more and look just like the nights in London, under the bombardments.

The Lieutenant's windows are as narrow as an arrow-loop in a castle wall. He looks out through the dirty panes, riddled with green and violet bubbles embedded in the rough glass. All he can see before him is the lane lost beneath the trees, like a lumberjack's path. Any trace of footsteps, either coming towards him or going away, has been washed away by the rain. He is alone, as though on a desert island.

The Lieutenant's supplies have been dwindling visibly now that the cleaning woman no longer comes.

And now he tests the sodden ground with his foot and sets out like someone who does not know what he is doing, letting his steps decide, leading him where they want to go, where he must go if he is to survive.

Once he has come to the end of the path and is facing the main road covered with puddles and mud, his feet no longer hold him up. He no longer has the courage to advance. The fear of facing up to this unknown village where he has never set foot freezes him where he stands. Besides, he is well aware of the true reason for his visit to the village. Though he will ask in a confident voice for milk, eggs, flour, tea, and potatoes, there is a serious risk that in the dim light of the shops he will arrive at the essential questions about the little girl that are tormenting him. Her name, her address, her house, and her garden. Her parents and her grandparents. Her friends. Her fields and her outbuildings. Her language and her religion. Her innocence, like a green fruit to be picked in the storm-furrowed countryside.

He retraces his steps. He goes back inside his house and heats up his last tin of Campbell's soup.

He will wait until there is nothing at all left on his shelf to drink or eat before he turns back to the village. That way he will be able to arrange matters so that his hunger and his thirst for the little girl are null and void, for long days yet to come.

III

THERE IS A RAINBOW, all its colours laid out clear and precise, while a second arc is forming behind the first, fragile as a glint in the water.

Clara is on her way to marry the English Lieutenant.

Dressed up and made-up, hat, gloves, and purse, perched on her high bicycle, Clara is making her way towards the luminous arches spread before her. She is paying close attention to the puddles that spatter her legs and are liable to ruin her wedding dress. Low branches drip onto her skirt and leave streaks of a deeper red than the rest of the dress.

Amid the imperceptible vibration of the day and the prism colours streaming before her, Clara pleads with a god she does not know, trembles before his hidden face, prays very softly that the Lieutenant will not take her as a cat takes his mate, sinking his fangs into her neck to keep her there beneath him while he tears her open.

The Lieutenant sees the red of Clara's dress coming in the distance, moving very quickly beneath the trees along the path.

When she is very close to him, all decked out and smeared with paint, her bicycle tossed into the grass, he does not recognize her at first. For a long moment he does nothing but look at her in amazement. He says:

"My God!"

And he rediscovers the fierce and joyous laughter of circus afternoons in his childhood.

"I was not expecting such a lovely clown!"

Clara does not stir under the laughter that tumbles onto her and insults her. Her high heels seem to put down roots in the floor. She has come here to be married to the Lieutenant and nothing and no one can prevent that from happening. Not laughter. Not tears. She is waiting for him to come back to his senses and stop laughing.

Now he becomes excessively grave, as if he were about to risk his soldier's life in a battle already lost. He takes the time to note meticulously everything about the little girl that bothers him. The dress, too long and out of date, streaked with grease, the high-heeled shoes, the little hat with its veil, the lipstick, and above all the ridiculous little gilt-clasped purse that she clutches as if her life depended on it. He doesn't know where to begin to rid her of all that, so that naked childhood will appear before him.

He wipes her cheeks and lips with a damp towel. He cannot bear Clara's eyes, which are open far too wide in her freshly washed face. He tells her to close them. He walks away from her in the room. He says some words in hushed tones, making them stand out clearly from one another, like pebbles he would fling into the water.

"Good girl, funny girl, good childish stuff, gorgeous gift from God to my poor soul."

The Lieutenant's words, incomprehensible, do not reach Clara, they seem to die along the way, having to cross the entire room in a foreign language before they reach her.

She has taken off her hat, her gloves, and her uncomfortable shoes. She is waiting for him to approach her. She has closed her eyes. She does what he has asked her to do.

In two strides he is beside her. He says again and again, "*Good girl, good girl,*" and strokes her frizzy hair as if he were trying to soothe a small animal which is at his mercy. The scent of Clara's hair is on the Lieutenant's hands. He sniffs his hands after they have left Clara's head. He is wild about its smell. Again he takes her tousled head in his hands. All the perfume of the little girl in the red dress rises to his face in warm exhalations, like the acrid odour that escapes from gamebags filled with wounded birds after a day of hunting, when the men return home staggering from a strange, cruel intoxication.

He sniffs her neck, under her arms, the folds of her dress, the hollow of her thighs. He drinks the tears from her blazing cheeks. He beseeches her to close her eyes and not to cry.

Amid a sound of old silk that rustles and tears under the Lieutenant's fingers, Clara is quickly undressed, having had nothing on her body but her bridal dress.

She does not open her eyes. She does not say a word. She lets him do what he wants to do. She learns from him what she was supposed to learn from him, for all eternity. Clara utters only one little cry, the cry of a dying child, when he enters her.

In the semi-darkness of the closed house they get their breath back, both of them, like castaways flung up onto the sand, with the ocean's backwash still beating inside them. For the Lieutenant, the sadness has already begun. Clara seeks him and calls him with her closed mouth. With the sensitive hands of a blind woman she tastes the sweetness of the Lieutenant's skin. He barely flinches under Clara's fingers, as if a light breath were brushing, in a dream, his sleeping body, his disarmed sex.

The kitchen table between them. The red-and-white checked oilcloth. The last package of crumbling biscuits. The boiling water poured over the last tea-leaves. The Lieutenant's provisions are exhausted.

They sip very pale tea from the chipped cups that came with the house. She has donned her rumpled dress again. Across from her there is a man dressed as a soldier who is drinking tea and crushing a biscuit in his saucer. A vague smile is frozen on his lips, is intended for no one, seems to drift in the stuffy air of the room with its drawn curtains, its locked door.

Already there is misunderstanding between them because of their different notions about the time that has been given them to be together, time that is ending and soon will be taken away.

She would like very much to stay with him in his cabin until the sun comes back and the roosters of Sainte-Clotilde and Valcour answer one another in the countryside, all together, upright on the first rays of dawn as on a high-wire, trying to outdo each other as they celebrate with a single raucous, strident fanfare the marriage of Clara and the English Lieutenant.

And she laughs because her notion is extravagant and fills her with joy. The Lieutenant will not know Clara's dream, any more than she will know his.

He waits for her to finish drinking her tea. He is filled with impatience and fear. His solitude is already there in the room, wary, only awaiting Clara's departure so it can take back the Lieutenant and close in around him.

He looks on his wrist for the time. He lifts the curtain at the window, sees that the daylight is fading, fears more than anything in the world being surprised with Clara here in his house.

"It's late, very late. You must go home now. You'll come back another time . . ."

He repeats "another time" and muffles his words so well that, later on, Clara will never be sure that she really heard them.

She picks up her hat, her purse, and her gloves, puts the high-heeled shoes on again. She stands facing him, expecting no improbable mercy from the Lieutenant. Perhaps she has already long been aware, in the darkness of her veins, of separation, of the brevity of love, its slight passage upon the world, like the swift shadow of a cloud across the fields.

Heels together, his tall body folded in two, he bows over Clara, kisses her hand, ceremonious and preoccupied. He says *sotto voce*, as if afraid of waking someone who is sleeping in the room:

"*Farewell, my love.*"

◂ AURÉLIEN IS OUTSIDE studying his garden that has been devastated by the storms. He is utterly unable to comprehend what is happening to him. He resembles a drunken man after a brawl, uncertain of what has gone on but struggling now to remain erect and ringing from head to foot from the blows he has received.

Perhaps he should not have tempted the devil and called out to his daughter after waiting for her such a long time, at the supper hour.

"You're home late!"

It was then that he saw appear suddenly on the mute face of his daughter, by way of response, something at once blazing and consumed that has been intolerable to her.

She nevertheless prepares everything as usual, despite her tardiness, cooking the potatoes and heating up the salt pork, before taking her place at the table. But suddenly, there across from Aurélien, is a strange woman who is his opposite, in place of the little girl he is accustomed to having in the house.

Late into the falling evening, Aurélien's gaze wanders here and there over everything that is broken, smashed, crushed, rotted all around him, from the fields to the garden, from the garden to the fields, without managing to settle down anywhere, as if he were searching vainly for the soul of the disaster that has gone astray in the countryside. But now Aurélien's gaze is suddenly fixed on a row of collapsed suns along the length of the henhouse. Amid the withered stems, flowers, and leaves, at the very heart of each great sunflower, the little burned face of his daughter endlessly appears and shows itself, for the damnation of Aurélien.

⬿ THIS MAN IS preparing to go away. He looks without seeing at the river fringed with foam that carries along broken branches, bits of wood, all kinds of nameless debris from its flooded banks.

The Lieutenant has packed his bags. It is the slack hour of the night. Long before dawn arrives and long after the day has ended. The dreary moment when nothing more will arrive. Save tedium. The middle of the darkness. The moment in sleep nearest to death. He must follow his own deepest law and flee before it is too late. So many hasty departures already in his life. So many little girls adored and then abandoned, amid the blood of the first embrace, while the fear of standing trial grows, before judges in wigs of white string.

The Lieutenant sets out, his pack on his back, carrying his suitcase. His heavy military shoes make a sucking sound on the waterlogged earth. Like a thief, he enters the opacity of night. At daybreak he will be thirty years old. His solitude on this deserted road fills him once more to the brim. Father, mother, masters, and governesses seem to be sleeping in the deepest part of his memory, carefully hiding their irritated faces in dark rooms cluttered with Victorian furniture. John Christopher Simmons might think he has had no childhood, no original curse, while a sentence from Rilke obsesses him and comes to him incessantly, assuring him that *while he was still a child they struck his face and called him cowardly.*

He would be content to mark his birthday by hitchhiking. But no car appears on the road. Too early or too late. He cannot see two steps ahead of him. Just enough ground to set his feet down, cautiously, between puddles. It is as foggy here as at the bottom of the sea. Who knows though what city, what unknown village might loom up at any moment at a turn in this endless road? The tall wet grass at the edge of the ditches, when his steps leave the path, grazes him as he passes, and the mingled perfumes stir all around him. The rain has started falling again, in slow, fine drops.

Very far away, in a landscape the Lieutenant has left behind on the bank of a wild river, in the heart of a frame house shut for the night, an adolescent is turning over as she slumbers. She finally fell asleep at dawn, exhausted as a child who has run all day into the wind and for whom tears are secretly lying in wait. Clara sleeps while the light spattering of rain on leaves and roof penetrates her night and gently lulls her, even slips into the strangest of her dreams.

The English Lieutenant strides away into the streaming countryside. Ahead of him, on the horizon, a vague glimmer beneath a mass of grey clouds. It resembles the day.